Dinosaur vs.
THE LIBRARY

BOB SHEA

Disney • Hyperion Books/New York

Text and Illustrations © 2011 by Bob Shea

All rights reserved. Published by Disney • Hyperion
Books, an imprint of Disney Book Group. No part
of this book may be reproduced or transmitted in
any form or by any means, electronic or mechanical,
including photocopying, recording, or by any
information storage and retrieval system, without
written permission from the publisher.

For information address Disney • Hyperion Books,
114 Fifth Avenue, New York, New York 10011-5690.

First Edition
10 9 8 7 6 5 4 3 2 1
F850-6835-5-11166
Printed in Singapore

ISBN 978-1-4231-3338-4
Reinforced binding

Visit www.disneyhyperionbooks.com

For Ryan, who loves the library

ROAR!

I'M A DINOSAUR!

ROaR!

I'm roaring to the library!

roar!

roar!

roar!

Dinosaur versus...

a cow!

moo.
moo.
moo.

ROAR!

ROAR!

Dinosaur versus...

baby chicks!

 peep!

peep!

peep!

peep!

 peep!

 peep!

 peep!

peep!

peep!

peep! peep!

peep! peep!

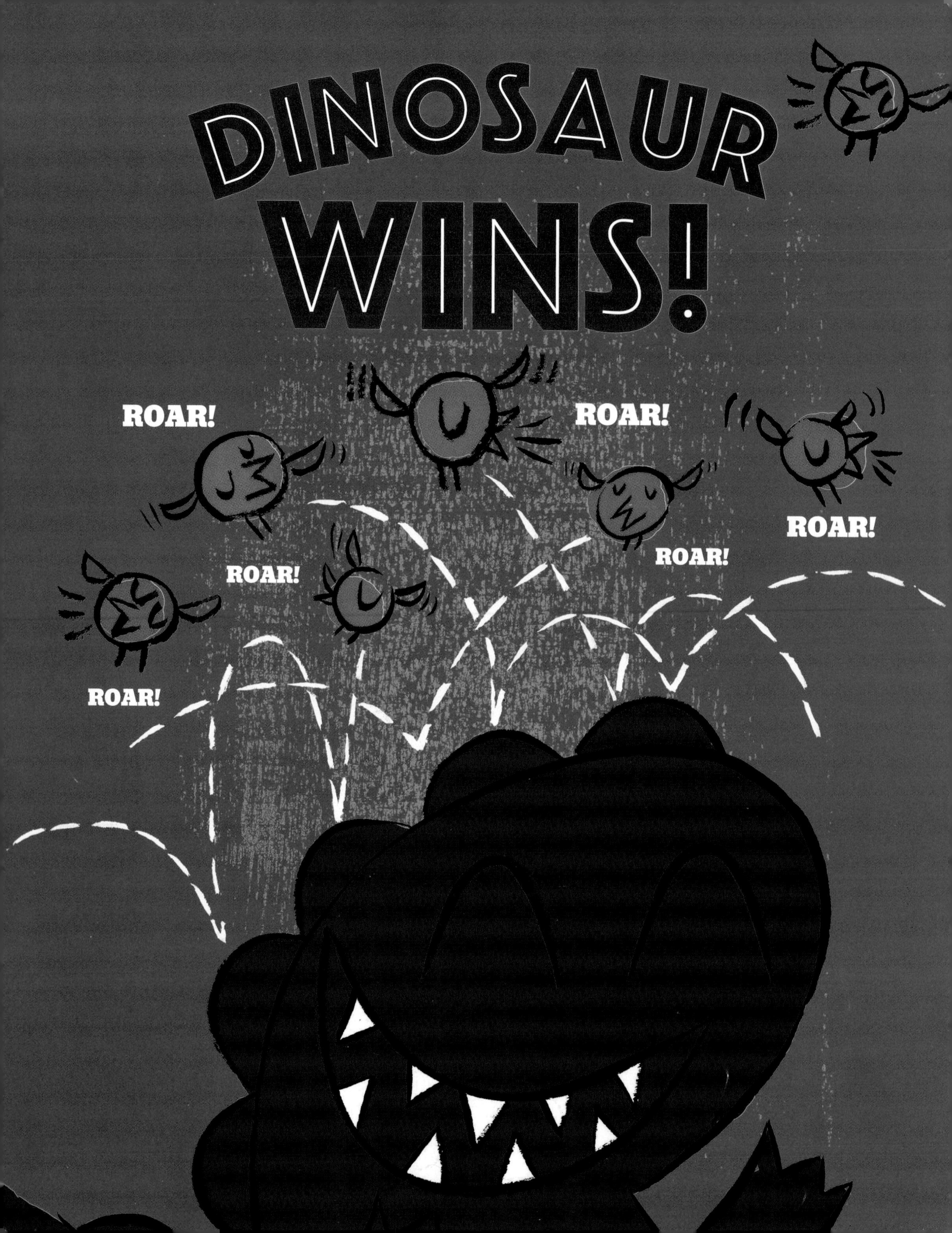
DINOSAUR WINS!
ROAR!
ROAR!
ROAR!
ROAR!
ROAR!
ROAR!

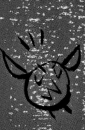

roar!

roar!

roar!

roar!

Dinosaur versus...

roar! roar! roar! roar! roar!

a shy turtle!

sigh

roar!

roar!

roar!

roar!

roar!

Dinosaur versus . . .

roar!

roar!

roar!

**Now Dinosaur will roar where
no one has roared before . . .**

BUT WAIT!

Can he do it?

Can Dinosaur not roar for a whole story?

The library wins!
Okay, they both win.